Splat the Cat
and the Pumpkin-Picking Plan

Based on the bestselling books by Rob Scotton

Cover art by Rick Farley

Text by Catherine Hapka

Interior illustrations by Loryn Brantz

HARPER FESTIVAL

An Imprint of HarperCollinsPublishers

HarperFestival is an imprint of HarperCollins Publishers.
Copyright © 2014 by Rob Scotton. All rights reserved.
Manufactured in China.
www.harpercollinschildrens.com
Library of Congress catalog card number: 2013956393
ISBN 978-0-06-211586-7

Typography by Rick Farley
14 15 16 17 18 SCP 10 9 8 7 6 5 4 3 2 1
❖
First Edition

Autumn was one of Splat's favorite seasons.

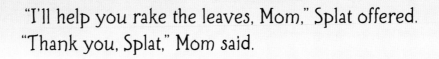

"I'll help you rake the leaves, Mom," Splat offered.
"Thank you, Splat," Mom said.

Splat was good at raking leaves. Seymour helped, too. Soon they'd made a huge pile.

Splat stared at the pile. Suddenly, he had a great idea. His tail wiggled wildly. . . .

SPLAT!

Leaves went flying everywhere!

Splat's mom sighed.

"I have an idea, Splat," she said. "Why don't you go to Farmer Patch's pumpkin patch? You can pick out a pumpkin to decorate and put on our porch."

Splat thought that sounded like a great idea.
"I'll pick the most perfect pumpkin ever," he promised.

Splat grabbed his wagon, and he and Seymour set off on their way.

Splat loved Farmer Patch's pumpkin patch. There was so much to see and do!

Farmer Patch's
PUMPKIN PATCH

He saw a very SCARY scarecrow.

He got lost in a hay-bale maze.

He tasted fresh
apple-and-fish cider.

Splat the Cat

HARPER FESTIVAL
An Imprint of HarperCollins Publishers
www.harpercollinschildrens.com
www.robscotton.com

Then Splat remembered: he was supposed to pick out the perfect pumpkin.
"The perfect pumpkin should be big, orange, and round," he told Seymour.

He found a pumpkin that was very round and very orange.
"Too small!" he announced.

The next pumpkin was big and orange.
"Not round enough," he told Seymour.

Seymour found a big, round pumpkin. "Not orange enough," Splat said.
Splat's tail wiggled wildly with worry. Would he ever find the perfect pumpkin?

MAZE

CIDER

But then Splat spotted another pumpkin. It was round. It was orange. It was the BIGGEST pumpkin in the place.

"Perfect!" Splat cried. "Mom will love this one!"
But there was one problem: how was Splat going to get the pumpkin home?
"This won't fit in my wagon," Splat said.

"I know," he said. "I'll roll it."

Splat rolled the pumpkin out of the gate.
He rolled it on to the road and down a hill.
"Whoa!" Splat cried.
Splat ran. The pumpkin rolled. The pumpkin
wouldn't stop no matter what Splat did!

"Help!" Splat cried.

and in between cars . . .

and right through his front gate!

Finally, the pumpkin stopped. Splat's mom smiled.
"Oh, Splat, it's perfect," she said. "Well done!"

Splat smiled back. "It was no trouble," he said. "No trouble at all."